Emily Mouse's
Christmas

Emily Mouse's Christmas

Vivian French

Illustrated by Mark Marshall

Orion
Children's Books

ORION CHILDREN'S BOOKS

First published in Great Britain in 2017
by Hodder and Stoughton

1 3 5 7 9 10 8 6 4 2

A CIP catalogue record for this book
is available from the British Library.

ISBN 978 1 5101 0177 7

Printed and bound in China

The paper and board used in this book are from well-managed forests
and other responsible sources.

Orion Children's Books
An imprint of
Hachette Children's Group
Part of Hodder and Stoughton
Carmelite House
50 Victoria Embankment
London EC4Y 0DZ

An Hachette UK Company
www.hachette.co.uk

www.hachettechildrens.co.uk

For Ivy, with lots of love from Gran xxx
To my little princess Bella, lots of love, MM

Emily Mouse woke up early.
"Hooray! Hooray! Tomorrow is
Christmas Day! I must get ready!"
And she jumped out of bed.

Emily washed her face . . .

and cleaned her teeth . . .

and brushed her whiskers.

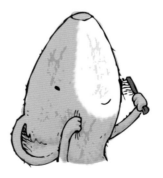

Then she ran into her kitchen.

"Fred and Sue and Jean and Little
Jim are coming for Christmas dinner.
Shall we have peanut butter biscuits,
or an extra cheesy cheese pie?"

"Cheese pie, I think. Everyone
likes that! Now, what do I need?"

Emily looked in her cupboard.

"Hmmm . . . I've got everything I need for biscuits. But an extra cheesy cheese pie is MUCH nicer – so I'll need more cheese. Lots more cheese! I'll have to go shopping."

"What else should I buy? Oh yes.
A little Christmas tree."

Cheese

More cheese

A little

Christmas Tree

"And then I'll come home and
make my pie. Goodness! I'm going to
be busy today!"

It was cold outside, so Emily put
on her warm winter coat and scarf.
Then she picked up her basket.
"Off I go!" she said.

But when Emily reached
the shops, she found they were
crowded.

The cheese shop had a long
queue outside, and she had to wait
for more than an hour.

"Oh dear," she said. "Maybe I should have done my shopping earlier. This isn't much fun . . . my paws are freezing!"

At last it was her turn. "Lots and
lots of cheese, please!" she said.

The shopkeeper shook his head. "Sorry, Emily Mouse. There's no cheese left."

Emily stared at him. "But how will I make my extra cheesy cheese pie? My friends are coming for Christmas dinner, and we must have something nice!"

"What about an apple pie?" the shopkeeper suggested.

"I suppose so," Emily said. "I'll go and buy some apples."

There was another long queue at the fruit shop.

Emily waited . . .

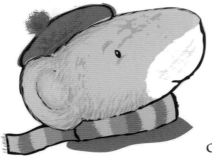

and waited . . .

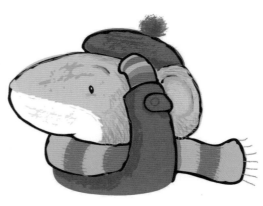

and waited.

"This isn't much fun at all,"
she said. "My paws are freezing,
and so are my ears!"

At last it was Emily's turn. "Lots of apples for an apple pie, please!"

"Sorry," said the shopkeeper. "No apples left. Only one bag of raisins."

"Oh dear." Emily looked sadly at the empty shelves. "I suppose I could make a raisin pie."

"Sounds fine to me," said the shopkeeper.

"Here you are . . . the last bag of raisins. Nothing left, now. Time to shut up my shop!"

Emily put the raisins into her basket, and went to look for a Christmas tree.

Christmas
Trees
THIS WAY

The streets were still very
crowded, and everyone was in a
rush. Emily was pushed this way
and that, and a very small mouse
ran over her toes with his scooter.

"Sorry! Sorry! Got to hurry!" he said, and scooted away.

"OUCH!!!" Emily rubbed her toes.

"I thought Christmas shopping would be fun, but it isn't. Not one bit! And aren't people meant to be kind and nice at Christmas? Huh! They aren't. They're HORRID!"

Quite soon it began to snow.
"Oh no!" said Emily.

"Now I'll be even colder!" She wrapped her scarf tightly round her neck, and hurried to the garden centre.

"I'll buy my little tree, and then I'll go home for a cup of tea," she said to herself.

There was only one Christmas tree left at the garden centre, and it was much **bigger** than Emily wanted.

"Last one," said the shopkeeper.
"Take it or leave it!"

LAST
ONE

Emily sighed. "I should DEFINITELY have done my shopping earlier."

"You can borrow a sleigh," the shopkeeper told her. "Bring it back after Christmas."

Emily began to drag the sleigh away. It was heavy, and it made her arms hurt.

She had to walk very slowly, and the snow kept blowing in her eyes.

"Oh dear oh dear oh DEAR,"
she said. "I do wish I was at home
in my cosy little house!"

She hadn't gone far when she heard someone crying.

She looked round, and saw the very small mouse with the scooter sitting on the path.

"What's the matter?" she asked.

The very small mouse sniffed loudly. "My mum sent me to buy a bag of raisins, but when I got to the fruit shop it was shut! So now me and my brothers and sisters won't have any Christmas pudding!"

"Oh dear," Emily said. She
looked at the very small mouse. His
nose was red, and his eyes were full
of tears.

"Do you have a lot of little
brothers and sisters?"
The very small mouse nodded.
"Yes." And he began to cry again.

Emily sighed, and looked at her
shopping basket.

"I've got a bag of raisins," she
said slowly. "And it's Christmas . . .
and Christmas is a time to be kind.
Here, little mouse, you can have
my raisins."

The very small mouse stopped
crying, and stared at her.
"Really? Don't you want them?"

"I wanted to make an extra cheesy cheese pie," Emily told him. "But there wasn't any cheese left in the cheese shop. I went to buy apples instead . . . but there weren't any apples, so I bought a bag of raisins. But it's all right, I can make peanut butter biscuits for my friends. Happy Christmas!"

The very small mouse clutched
the bag. "THANK YOU!" he said.
"We don't like cheese or apples in
our house, but we LOVE Christmas
pudding! Thank you SO MUCH!"

And he scooted away as fast as
he could go.

Emily watched him disappear,
then put her basket on her arm and
picked up the rope for the sleigh.

"One two three, HEAVE!" she
said. "One two three, HEAVE!
Come on, Emily! You can do it!"

Emily was very tired when she got home. She put the tree in the corner of her sitting room, then sat down.

"I'm too tired to make biscuits tonight," she said. "I'll make them in the morning."

She gave a huge yawn. "In fact, I think I'll go to bed right now. Oh dear . . . I hope it's a better day tomorrow."

RAT A TAT TAT!

It was early on Christmas morning, and Emily woke up with a jump. "Who's that?"

RAT A TAT TAT!

Emily jumped out of bed
and ran to open the door in her
pyjamas.

Outside the door was the very small mouse, with his scooter and a big basket.

"My mum sent me," he said. "I've got something for you, to say thank you for the raisins." He gave Emily the basket.

"Happy Christmas!" he said and he scooted away.

Emily took the basket indoors, and opened it. It was full of cheese . . . lots and lots of cheese!

"Oh, hurrah!" Emily's eyes shone. "Now I can make an extra cheesy cheese pie for my friends. It'll be a lovely Christmas after all!"

And it was.

Emily's friends said her extra
cheesy cheese pie was DELICIOUS …

. . . and when six little mice came
round to sing carols outside the
door that evening, Emily knew it
was the best Christmas ever.

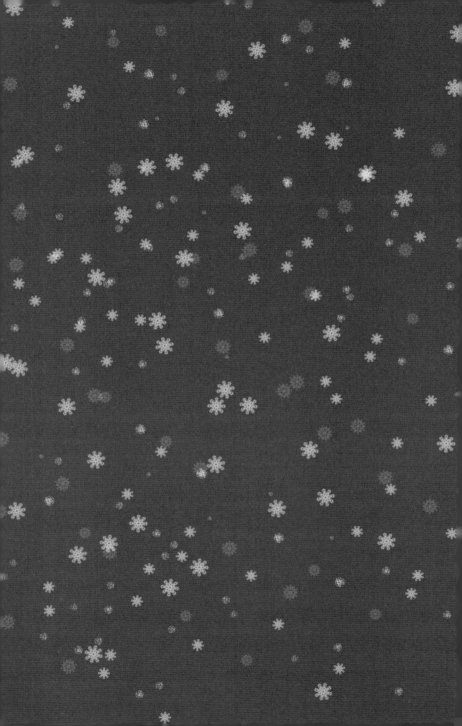